D1529211

FiGMENT

JOURNEY INTO IMAGINATION, VOLUME 3

 Spotlight

Disney KINGDOMS

MARVEL

ABDOPUBLISHING.COM

Reinforced library bound edition published in 2016 by Spotlight,
a division of ABDO, PO Box 398166, Minneapolis, Minnesota 55439.
Spotlight produces high-quality reinforced library bound editions for
schools and libraries. Published by agreement with Marvel Characters, Inc.

Printed in the United States of America, North Mankato, Minnesota.
092015
012016

THIS BOOK CONTAINS
RECYCLED MATERIALS

marvelkids.com
© 2016 MARVEL

Elements based on Figment © Disney.

CATALOGING-IN-PUBLICATION DATA

Zub, Jim.
 Figment : journey into imagination / writer, Jim Zub ; artist, Filipe Andrade
and John Tyler Christopher. -- Reinforced library bound edition.
  p. cm. (Figment : journey into imagination)
"Marvel."
Summary: Dive into a steampunk fantasy story exploring the never-before-
revealed origin of the inventor known as Dreamfinder, and how one little
spark of inspiration created a dragon called Figment.
ISBN 978-1-61479-445-5 (vol. 1) -- ISBN 978-1-61479-446-2 (vol. 2) -- ISBN
978-1-61479-447-9 (vol. 3) -- ISBN 978-1-61479-448-6 (vol. 4) -- ISBN 978-1-
61479-449-3 (vol. 5)
1. Figment (Fictitious character)--Juvenile fiction. 2. Dragons--Juvenile
fiction. 3. Adventure and adventures--Juvenile fiction. 4. Graphic novels-
-Juvenile fiction. I. Andrade, Filipe, illustrator. II. Christopher, John Tyler,
illustrator. III. Title.
741.5--dc23

2015955126

Spotlight

A Division of ABDO
abdopublishing.com

Journey Into Imagination
Part Three

JIM ZUB writer
FILIPE ANDRADE artist
JEAN-FRANCOIS BEAULIEU colorist
VC'S JOE CARAMAGNA letterer

JOHN TYLER CHRISTOPHER cover artist

JIM CLARK, BRIAN CROSBY
ANDY DIGENOVA, TOM MORRIS
& JOSH SHIPLEY
walt disney imagineers

MARK BASSO assistant editor
BILL ROSEMANN editor

AXEL ALONSO editor in chief
JOE QUESADA chief creative officer
DAN BUCKLEY publisher

special thanks to
DAVID GABRIEL

FIGMENT

Blarion Mercurial, a young inventor at the **Academy Scientifica-Lucidus,** has been using his imaginative talents to develop an alternative energy source. His creation, the **Integrated Mesmonic Converter,** designed to form energy out of pure thought, had a few hiccups. The first trial run blew up in his face. The second brought to life a figment of his imagination—a purple dragon called, appropriately enough, **Figment.** The latest attempt opened a portal that pulled Blair and Figment into another world entirely.

Chairman Illocrant, Blair's boss, was none-too-happy with these results. In trying to shut down the chaotic machine, Illocrant inadvertently summoned the **Singular,** robotic Commander of Clockwork Control, who now looks to impose his own brand of structured rule on England.

Meanwhile, Blair and Figment explored the dream-like world they're now stuck in and made friends with a playful creature called **Chimera.** Chimera's loud roars attracted the negative attention of the Sound Sprites, who promptly swooped in to confront the group. Chimera fled. The **Sound Sprites** conjured up a net from pure sound to capture Blair and Figment.

They're probably *not* going to be friends.

This whole thing is both bewildering and astounding, Figment.

The energy I tapped into with my Mesmonic Converter opened a portal to this incredible place, but the locals consider us... well, I'm not sure *what* they consider us.

A *threat?* An *annoyance?*

They didn't hurt us, so maybe it's a *misunderstanding.*

The next time one zips by we'll just explain that they've made a *mistake.*

Be careful, stranger.

Sound sprites don't make mistakes...or at least, that's what they *tell* themselves.

Everything they do is about keeping *"harmony,"* and they're convinced you're *"off key."*

I'm confused...aren't you *one* of them?

Not anymore.

What's your *name?*

They call me *"Fye the Flawed."*

They locked you up too?

Yes.

It's called *"isolating bad audio."*

My name's *Blair*. This is *Figment*.

We're *friendly!*

We came to this world quite by *accident* so this is all quite confusing. Any information on where we are or what this is all about would be most appreciated.

The world is broken up into regions. Each one is ruled differently.

This *audio acreage* is controlled by *sound sprites.*

They extract notes from sound sap and then *"play"* them to make new things.

Everything here comes from sound.

So *neat!* Why aren't you doing that too?

Like I said, I've got *"bad audio"*... *Watch.*

ZBZBZBZBZB

See?

I don't talk like the others and my wings don't work right. Instead of *making* things, I'm *breaking* things...turning stuff into bad music.

Everything I do turns out *wrong*.

I don't fit in.

÷sigh÷ I know *that* feeling...

Don't give up, Fye, my friend!

You said there were *other* places, right?

We'll find a way out and go somewhere you'll be *appreciated!*

Sure, but *where?*

The Color Wheel? Mathmagic Land? No one goes to the Nightmare Nation by *choice...*

Blair's from somewhere called *"Earth."* It seems nice.

Yes, Earth sounds great right about now.

We have to get back there as soon as possible.

Chairman Illocrant is probably filling out my *termination papers* as we speak...

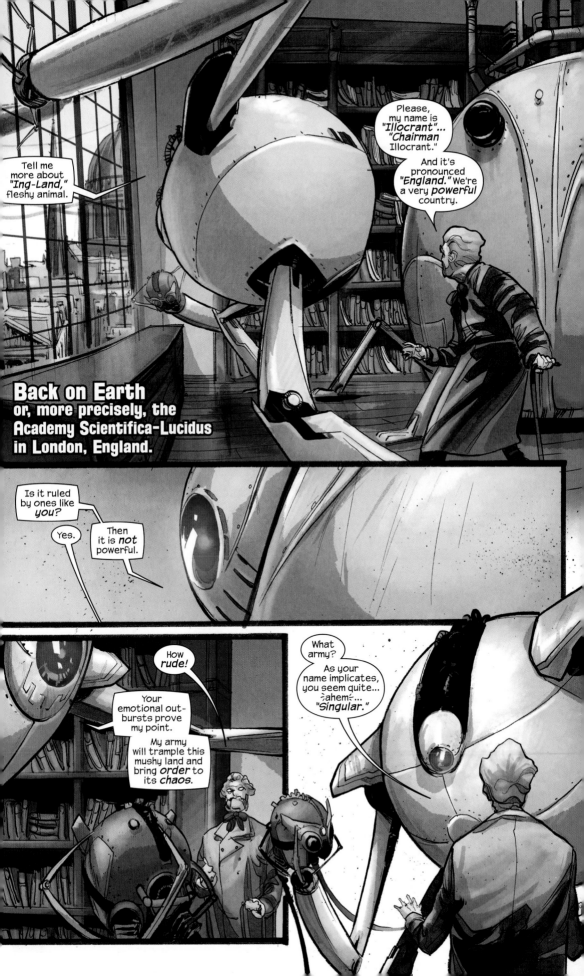

KRAKOOM

Oh, no...what... what have I *done*?

You have built a *bridge*, Mr. Chair-Man.

A bridge to the Clockwork Capital.

My troops are fearless, tireless, *efficient*...

...and this shall be the staging ground for *absolute order*.

**Early Figment and Dreamfinder character designs
for the Journey Into Imagination ride by X Atencio**

Artwork courtesy of Walt Disney Imagineering Art Collection